ORLANDO THE ZOO SQUIRREL

GOES TO THE COUNTRY

To My Dad, Verner R Love,
who always believed in me and loved to read and draw.
–Mary Fran

To Grandma Dixie,
for always believing in me and my art.
–Amanda

IBSN: 978-0-578-52506-8

This is
a story
about Orlando
the Zoo Squirrel.

Orlando lived in the City Zoo with his big and
wonderful family whom he loved very much.
His mother, Dixie, loved to cook for the family.
His father, Randy, played the piano while the
whole family sang their favorite squirrel songs.

Orlando loved his brothers and little sister. He played with them in the big, leafy trees of the City Zoo. The brothers ran and leapt across the branches, high above their friends in the zoo. When their little sister, Wanda, wanted to play, they took her outside for hide-and-seek!

Orlando's brothers, Nico, Sammy, and Jack loved to watch the popcorn cart. Spilt popcorn at the Zoo made the squirrels very happy!

Orlando loved to visit his Zoo friends and find out all the Zoo news.

"Hello cubs!" Orlando said to the baby lions, "You're growing up so fast!"

"Rawr!" the cubs growled, "we're going to be so big!"

"Who's this?" Papa Lion bellowed.

"This is Orlando the Zoo Squirrel!" the cubs exclaimed, "he's our friend!"

"Well, he looks more like a little snack to me," Papa Lion grunted,

"Come now cubs and let me teach you lion things!"

Orlando jumped up and scampered away.

He did not want to be a lion snack!

Next, Orlando visted the wolves' forest.
His parents told him to stay high in the trees because
you never know what a wolf might do!
"Hello wolf," Orlando said, "you look very happy today!"
"Yes, Orlando!" said the wolf, "tonight is a full moon
and I'm looking forward to howling with my pack.
You know, wolves are the same family as dogs
and we love to howl at the moon!"
"That sounds fun! Well, try not to wake me up
with your howling!" And with that,
Orlando scurried away.

Orlando always stopped to see the zebras in the afternoon when they woke from their naps.

"Hello Zebras!" Orlando called, "Wait, where are you?"

"Oh, hello there Orlando," the Zebras yawned, "I bet you can't find us!
Our stripes hide us in the grass."

"There you are!" Orlando laughed when he spotted them hiding.

"No one can beat us at hide and seek!"

"I guess so!" Orlando said, "Maybe we can play later!
For now, I'm on my way to
see the elephants!"

Orlando hurried to the elephant house and hopped onto momma elephant's trunk.

"Hey everyone, look who's here!" momma elephant called to the herd, "it's Orlando!"

"Hello elephants!" Orlando exclaimed. "Why is it that you're always together when I visit?"

"Well, that's what elephants do!" she laughed,

"we stick with our families and take care of each other."

"That is so cool!" Orlando cried, "I love my family, too.
I think I'll head back home now and see them."

Orlando was looking forward to getting back to his family and the tree house. But he was very tired from visiting all his friends. And that's when he saw a truck with a very, very comfy looking blanket in the back.

Before he knew it the little squirrel was falling into a very, very
sound sleep and nothing could wake him up.
Not the zookeeper putting his bag in the truck,
not the engine starting up,
and not even the sound of the highway traffic.
Orlando was sound asleep
and far, far away from home.

When Orlando awoke from his nap, he jumped
out of the truck and looked around.
What he saw filled
his eyes with tears.
He was not in the
Zoo anymore!

Then Orlando saw two elderly squirrels walking down the path, hand in hand.

"Hello," he whimpered, "my name is Orlando and I live in the Zoo. I think I'm very far away from my home."

"Hello there," one of the squirrels said softly, "my name is Mr. Clarence Duffy and this is Mrs. Duffy. We live in the neighborhood, but I don't know of any zoos around here."

"Oh," Orlando sighed, "I must be a long way from home," a tiny tear rolled down his cheek.

"Don't be sad, dear," Mrs. Duffy cooed, "Amelda will help you. She said she knows everything! Look for the blue house on the left and Amelda will be on her porch."

Orlando ran quickly to the blue house and saw
a fluffy dog on the porch.
She was wearing a very fancy collar
that said "Amelda" in diamonds.
"Excuse me" Orlando squeaked,
"are you a wolf?"
"Of course not! I'm no wolf,"
Amelda said in a most fussy voice!
"I am a poodle. Poodles are the best and
most smart dogs in the world."
"Oh," Orlando mumbled, "I have wolf friends
at the Zoo. They are very smart, too!"
"Not as smart as poodles!" huffed Amelda.
"Do you like my emerald earrings?"
Amelda seemed too interested in herself
to be of any help to Orlando,
so he scurried away.

At the next house, he spotted a small, yellow, furry cat in the window. "Hello," Orlando called, "are you a lion? I'm not supposed to go near the lions because they might eat me!"
"My name is Lisa. I won't hurt you," she hissed.
"Come play with me!" She showed a gigantic smile with very, very large, white teeth.
Orlando knew not to trust this cat. She might not be a lion, but she did not look friendly!

Orlando wandered sadly around the neighborhood
until he came to a large red barn,
with a giant black and white animal grazing in the field.
"Wow!" Orlando exclaimed, "are you a hippo?"
"My goodness! Of course not!" cried the cow,
"I am a cow, not a hippo! My name is Marianna.
Haven't you ever seen a cow before?"

"My name is Orlando and I live in the Zoo," he said.
"We have hippos and elephants that are very big,
but I've never seen a cow before."
Marianna laughed. "I live on this farm and graze
on the grass with my friends. Would you like
to live here on the farm with us?"
"Your farm is beautiful! But I miss my family
and friends at the Zoo very much,"
Orlando tried to hold back a tear.
"Don't cry little one!" Marianna said kindly,
"maybe the deer will help. They travel all over the land
in herds and work together to help all the animals.
If you go into the woods, the deer will see you
and help you find the Zoo and your family."

... and there was the deer, standing right in front of Orlando!

"Hello there, little one," The deer said softly. "My name is Abdo.
Are you Orlando, the squirrel from the zoo?
Your family asked all the animals to look for you."
"I am Orlando," he whispered,
still a little afraid of the towering creature.
"Can you help me get back to the Zoo and my family?"
Abdo nodded his head, with its gigantic antlers, "hop on."

The deer led him into the neighborhood, and there was the very same truck
where Orlando had fallen asleep the day before.
"Just climb into the back and stay very quiet." Abdo said with a smile.
"In a little while, the man will drive you back to the Zoo,
and your family will be waiting for you."
Then, before Orlando knew it,
the deer was gone

Orlando climbed back into the truck and watched
the neighborhood slowly fade into the distance.
Orlando was finally home at the Zoo!

Orlando ran back to his tree as fast as he could to find his family.
Waiting at the door was his mother, and she welcomed him home with a gigantic hug!
His whole family was very, very happy to have him back.
So happy that they gave him a big bowl of popcorn to celebrate.

Orlando told his family all about the neighborhood and the new friends he had made there. He also told them about Abdo, the deer, and how kind he was.

"Why did Mr. Abdo help me, father?" Orlando asked.

"Because the animals care about each other," father said.

"The world is very big, but it is also very small. We have a duty to care for each other, and the deer know how important that is. We're very grateful to have you home, safe and sound, all because of Mr. Abdo."

That night, the Zoo animals were all
very happy to have Orlando home.
Everyone thanked the deer and
promised to always take care of
each other, just as Mr. Abdo
had for their zoo friend.